counting
comic
history puzzle
electronic craft sticker
spot-the-difference
scary
picture

This book belongs to

BEN, Bella, and...

REELCY

D0245905

**For Gail and for Friendly,
her fondly remembered dog.**

OXFORD
UNIVERSITY PRESS

Great Clarendon Street, Oxford OX2 6DP.
United Kingdom

Oxford University Press is a department of the University of Oxford.
It furthers the University's objective of excellence in research,
scholarship, and education by publishing worldwide

Oxford is a registered trade mark of Oxford University Press
in the UK and in certain other countries

Text and illustrations © Richard Byrne 2016

The moral rights of the author/illustrator have been asserted
Database right Oxford University Press (maker)

Photographs: Shutterstock.com/Mayokova pages 9 and 11/Ruth Black pages 9 and 11/
Kesu pages 8 and 10/ Pius Lee page 14/ Oleg Golovnev page 15/ George Filyagin
pages 22 and 23

First published in 2016

British Library Cataloguing in Publication Data
Data available

ISBN: 978-0-19-274318-3 (paperback)

10 9 8 7 6 5 4 3 2 1

Printed in China
Paper used in the production of this book is a natural, recyclableproduct made from
wood grown in sustainable forests.The manufacturing process conforms to the
environmental regulations of the country of origin.

Visit www.richardbyrne.co.uk

We're in the wrong book!

Richard BYRNE

OXFORD
UNIVERSITY PRESS

Bella and Ben were jumping down the street, from one side of the book . . .

. . . to the other.

I win!

Then Bella's dog joined in . . .

'Where's my dog?' said Bella.

9 Pencils

'Where
are we?'
said Ben.

10 Lollipops

'We're in the wrong book!'

9 Pencils

'Well let's jump back into
the right book,' said Ben.

But they jumped into . . . .

10 Lollipops

. . . somebody else's COMIC book!

Yikes!

Eeek!

'We're trying to get back to our own book,' explained Ben and Bella.

'We know someone who can help,' said Mouse. 'Follow us.'

LIBRARY

Ben and Bella described their book to the lovely librarian.

'It has tall buildings . . .'

'. . . and an enormous dog.'

'I know the book,' she said.

'It's through there.'

'I hope she's right,' said Bella.

'What does it all mean?' asked Ben.

'I think it says walk this way,' said Bella.

But things just got more and more puzzling.

And when Bella thought she had found a path that would lead them back to their book . . .

. . . instead it led them to the door of an old cottage in the middle of a wood. Ben and Bella went inside . . .

. . . where an odd-looking lady invited them to stay for dinner. 'Thank you but we really must get back to our own book,' said Bella. Ben thought he could see a way back . . .

... suddenly Ben and Bella were in a book full of instructions. 'I suppose we could follow them,' said Bella.

1. Take a piece of rectangular paper ...

It doesn't have to be this huge!

2. ... and fold it in half.

3. Fold a top corner towards the centre ...

4. ... and then the other.

5. Fold up the flap at the bottom.

6. Turn over and repeat.

7. Fold both corners of the flap inwards.

8 Turn over and repeat.

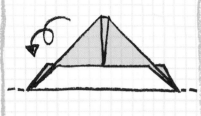

9 Hold the bottom-centre fold of each side and pull outwards . . .

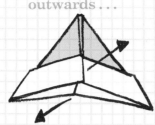

10 . . . and press flat.

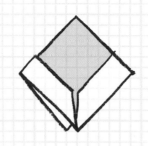

11 Fold the bottom triangle up.

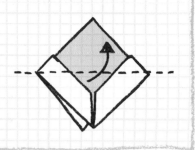

12 Turn over and repeat.

15 . . . and your boat is ready to sail!

13 Hold the bottom-centre fold of each side and pull outwards. Press flat.

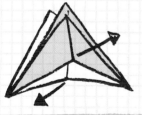

14 Hold the top-outer corners and pull outwards . . .

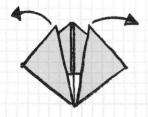

'Book ahoy!' said Ben.

'The WRONG book ahoy!' grumbled Bella. 'And now we're stuck in it!'

So they stuck themselves in a hot-air balloon as it lifted up, up, and away.

The balloon landed
in just the right spot . . .

Can you spot ten differences between these two pictures?

. . . for spotting
a very helpful sign.

THIS WAY

N-n-not a helpful sign at all. We're in a dark, scary book with a m-m-monster!
I have an idea. Quick! Follow me.

And they both jumped through
the monster-shaped hole.

'Yay!' said Bella.
'We're back in our book!'

When Ben and Bella came back to fix the hole in their book there was no sign of the monster.

'Thank goodness!' said Bella. 'Now, where's my dog?'